The Wonderful BOOK

LEONID GORE

The Wonderful Book

SCHOLASTIC INC.
New York Toronto London Auckland
Sydney Mexico City New Delhi Hong Kong

ISBN 978-0-545-41457-9

12 11 10 9 8 7 6 5 4 3 2 1   11 12 13 14 15 16/0

Printed in the U.S.A.   08

First Scholastic paperback printing, November 2011

The text type was set in Gill Sans Bold
and Gill Sans Extra Bold.
The display type was set in F 2 F Tagliatelle Bold.
The art was created using watercolor and ink on textured paper.
Art direction and book design by Marijka Kostiw

For

book lovers everywhere,

big and small!

—L.G.

One sunny day,

a rabbit saw something wonderful
while hopping about in the forest.

"What is this?" he asked.

"It will make a cozy little house for me!"

So he wriggled inside,

and there he stayed until . . .

. . . a big growly bear came along!

"Grrrrrrrrrrrr!" said the bear.

"That's mine!

It will make a pretty hat for me!"

And he put it on his head and
strutted happily around the forest.

But the bear lost his hat while he
stopped for a snack . . .

. . . and soon a family of mice found it.
"What is this?"
"What is this?"
"What is this?" asked the mice.
"It will make a perfect table for us!"

So they ate their dinner
and scampered away.

At sunset, a tired little fox came along.

"What is this?" asked the tired little fox.

"It will make a comfortable bed for me."

Soon, he fell fast asleep
and had sweet, happy dreams all night long.

The next morning, a hungry little worm slithered by when he spied something in the distance.

So he hurried over to take a closer look.

But worms are very slow.

It took him till noon to get there.

"What a tasty-looking flower," said the little worm.

"It will make a delicious lunch for me!"

But just as he was about to take a big bite . . .

. . . along came a curious boy.

"Look at this!" said the boy. "It's a book!

I wonder what it's about!"

So he sat down and began to read.

Soon, everyone gathered around to listen.

They listened as he read about a little rabbit
and a big grumpy bear. He read about some
hungry mice and a tired little fox.

He read about a little pink worm and
a curious little boy, and much, much more!

"What a wonderful book!" said the boy.

And everybody agreed.